THE MYSTERY OF THE LOST MINE

created by
GERTRUDE CHANDLER WARNER

Illustrated by Charles Tang

ALBERT WHITMAN & Company
Morton Grove, Illinois

ISBN 0-8075-5428-6

3 5 7 9 10 8 6 4 2

Printed in the U.S.A.

Contents

CHAPTER 1

The New Boxcar

"Turn left," said Henry Alden. Leaning forward from the passenger seat, he pointed at a graveled road. "RV Haven should be about two miles down this road."

"Roger," said Grandfather as he steered the big mobile home off the main highway.

Benny looked up from the map Henry had given him to fold. He sat on the bench seat behind his big brother.

"Roger?" he repeated. "Henry's name isn't Roger."

Grandfather laughed. "That's navigator

1

talk. Henry has been an excellent one since we left Greenfield."

"What's a nav — ?" six-year-old Benny began.

"A direction finder," answered Jessie, who was twelve, from the opposite bench. She was used to her little brother's questions. She glanced around the kitchenette. "Since we're almost there, we'd better straighten up."

"I'll put my drawing things away," offered Violet. She packed up her tablet and pens and stowed them in the cubby beneath the kitchen table. Ten-year-old Violet Alden loved to draw.

"Are there any more sandwiches?" asked Benny. He was always hungry.

Jessie wiped crumbs from the counter. "Oh, Benny! I just cleaned the kitchen."

"We'll be there in ten minutes," Grandfather told Benny, glancing in the rearview mirror. "And then we can have dinner in the restaurant."

Violet joined Jessie on the bench behind the driver's seat. "The campground has a restaurant?" she asked.

Most of the campgrounds across the country had only trailer hookups for power. Violet, Jessie, and Henry had taken turns fixing light meals.

"This place is supposed to have everything," said Henry, who was fourteen. "A pool, a recreation center, riding stables nearby — "

"RV Haven is like a little town, right in the Arizona desert," Grandfather added.

"Eight minutes," called out Benny. "And then we'd better be there!"

Everyone laughed.

Violet gazed out the big picture window at the passing scenery of cactus and rocks. She couldn't wait to take pictures with the camera Grandfather had given her. For a ten-year-old, she was a pretty good artist and photographer.

At last the RV lumbered under a tall wooden arch with "RV Haven" spelled out in horseshoes.

"We're here!" exclaimed Jessie. She clung to the back of Benny's seat.

Grandfather pulled the mobile home in

front of a small wooden building marked "Office."

"I'll be right back," he said, opening the door. "I have to sign in and find out where we can park the RV."

"Five minutes!" Benny sang after him. But he didn't care if Grandfather took an extra minute or two. After more than a week on the road, they had finally reached their destination.

"I can't believe we're here," Henry said, echoing Benny's thought. "It seems like a month since we left Greenfield — "

"And started west in Mr. McCrae's RV," Jessie filled in.

Gerald McCrae and Grandfather had been friends forever. When Grandfather offered to help work on Mr. McCrae's cabin in Arizona, Mr. McCrae asked Mr. Alden to drive his RV out.

"Aren't you glad Grandfather thought we should come along on this trip?" Henry asked.

"I'm glad he did," said Violet. "We've seen practically the whole country!"

"The RV is neat," Benny put in. He jumped out of his seat and ran around the kitchenette, then he stopped for a moment. "What does RV stand for anyway?"

"It stands for recreational vehicle," said Jessie.

The RV was truly a miniature house on wheels. Benches behind the driver's and passengers' seats folded down into bunk beds. The dining table stood between the benches. The kitchenette was outfitted with a tiny sink, refrigerator, and stove.

Behind the kitchen was a sitting area with comfortable chairs. At the very back were the bathroom with a shower and a small, separate bedroom.

"It *is* neat," Henry agreed. "Like a brand-new boxcar."

The Alden children used to live alone in a boxcar after their parents had died. But then their grandfather found them and gave them a wonderful home in Greenfield.

"Well, our old boxcar is in Grandfather's back yard," Jessie reminded them. "The *new* boxcar is only ours until Grandfather helps

Mr. McCrae finish building his cabin."

"And I hope that'll be a long, *long* time!" Benny declared.

At that moment, Grandfather returned with a packet of papers he placed on the dashboard.

"Block D, Number Two," he announced, starting the engine. "That's our parking spot. Should be just ahead."

Recreational vehicles, Jessie noticed, came in all shapes and sizes. Theirs was one of the biggest on the road.

"Here's Two-D," Henry said, as Grandfather maneuvered the mobile home onto the paved pad. "I'll help hook up."

"Me, too!" Benny leaped out after them. At every campground stop, he proudly helped connect the RV to water, sewer, and electricity lines. Jessie and Violet stayed in the RV.

Each RV site held four vehicles. Block D contained three trailers. The Alden RV filled the last slot.

The other three units were occupied by a

shiny, oblong trailer; a fair-size RV with stickers all over the rear bumper; and an RV that was even bigger and sleeker than the Aldens'.

"Wow!" Jessie exclaimed softly as she and Violet looked out their RV's window. "I wonder who lives in *that* one."

Just then, the RV's door burst open and Benny thundered up the steps.

"Come on!" he called. "Time to eat!"

Grandfather smiled. "That boy will never be late to a meal," he told the girls as he locked the door behind them.

Henry waited for them at the entrance to the restaurant. "The Chuck Wagon," he said, indicating the branded sign. "Neat name, huh? There's also a store in the back."

A cowbell clanged cheerfully as they entered.

"Let's sit there," Benny said, pointing to a red leather booth.

"Order anything you like," Grandfather told them. "I'm going back to the office to call Gerald McCrae and let him know we're here and ready to get to work on his cabin."

When he left, a dark-haired woman with hard eyes came over with menus.

"Are you the campers in Two-D?" the woman asked without even saying hello first.

"Yes," Jessie replied. "We're the Aldens. I'm Jessie."

"Janine Crawford," the waitress replied shortly. "I run the restaurant and the store in back."

The woman shifted her weight impatiently. "If you all know what you want — "

Since they were all hungry, they ordered quickly: grilled cheese and fries for Violet, hamburgers for Henry, Benny, and Grandfather, and a taco salad for Jessie.

As Janine barked the order to the cook in the back, a thin, blond man came in. Henry admired his cowboy boots and engraved silver belt buckle.

The young man tipped his gray cowboy hat and walked over to their table. "Howdy, pardners. I'm Tom Parker."

"I'm Henry Alden and this is my brother, Benny, and my sisters, Jessie and Violet."

"You're the folks in Two-D," Tom guessed. "Your first time to Arizona?"

The children nodded.

"It's so pretty," Violet said. "In a different sort of way."

"The territory is pretty rugged all right." Tom brought over a water pitcher and four glasses.

"Do you work here?" Benny wanted to know. He was thinking about becoming a cowboy.

Turning a chair around backward, Tom sat down. "Yeah, I'm jack-of-all-trades around here."

"And master of none," Janine snapped as she set down a loaded tray. "Did you check the pool filter? And rake the gravel by the rec center?"

"Not yet." When Janine left, Tom said with a broad wink, "Well, I guess I better hit the trail. According to her, I have a lot of work to do. See you around."

The Aldens dug into their food.

"I wonder why Janine is so grouchy," Jessie said.

"If I owned a restaurant, I wouldn't be grouchy," said Benny.

Just then the door opened and several people came in. A man, woman, and a boy about Henry's age sat in the booth across from the Aldens. The boy smiled.

"Hi," he said. "I'm Luis Garcia. You're the people — "

" — in Two-D," Henry finished with a laugh. He introduced his sisters and brother. "I guess everyone is known around here by their RV."

Luis's father smiled. "Ours is the well-traveled one."

Violet remembered all the stickers on the back bumper of the trailer parked directly in front of theirs.

"Would you like to sit with us?" Henry offered.

"Luis, why don't you join the young people?" Luis's mother urged. "You haven't met many children on this trip."

Luis scooted into the Aldens' booth. "How long are you staying?"

Henry explained about Grandfather's working on Mr. McCrae's cabin. "We could be here a week or so."

Luis nodded. "We've been here a week already. My parents are geologists. We are on vacation, but a vacation for my parents means rocks, rocks, and more rocks!"

"Do you collect rocks, too?" Jessie wondered.

"I'm a rock hound, yes. It's in the blood, I think."

"Who are in the other trailers?" Henry asked. "Are they in here now?"

Luis lowered his voice. "Yes. The silver Airstream is owned by that man." He nodded toward a tall, thin man who slouched over a cup of coffee. "His name is Mr. Tobias. He's been here the longest, about a month. He stays in his trailer most of the time."

"Why would anyone stay inside all day in a great place like this?" asked Violet.

Luis shrugged. "The couple in the booth

over there own the big, fancy mobile home parked next to you. They are Mr. and Mrs. Clark."

Jessie had noticed that couple. They were very young and flashily dressed. Right now they were both laughing and joking with Tom Parker, who had come back inside.

"You two ought to book an evening hike with me," Tom was telling them. "The desert is a mighty fine sight at night."

"We'd love to, wouldn't we, Jim?" Mrs. Clark said to her husband.

Mr. Clark smiled at his wife. "If Caitie wants to hike in the desert, we'll go."

"Good! We'll set a date." Tom slapped their table in parting and came over to the Aldens. "Hey, I see you met my buddy Luis. Luis here can swap almost as many tall tales as I can."

Luis gave a tight smile. "Not quite, Mr. Parker."

Jessie wondered why Luis didn't seem to like the young cowboy. Tom seemed very friendly.

Tom splashed water into their glasses, his mood suddenly changing.

"Listen, you kids. Water is a serious business in Arizona. Don't ever be without it. The desert can be a dangerous place, you know."

"Dangerous?" Benny asked, looking a little frightened.

"How do you mean, Mr. Parker?" Henry asked.

"Just be careful," Tom said, and stalked off without another word.

CHAPTER 2

A New Adventure

"Boy, it sure gets dark out here," Benny commented as he reached for a handful of popcorn.

"Quiet, too," said Jessie. Then she added with a laugh, "Except for Benny's chewing!"

The Aldens had just finished taking turns showering in the RV's tiny bathroom. Now they were sitting around, munching popcorn. Outside the big picture windows, they could see a few lights from the campground. Beyond, the desert was inky black.

"What do you suppose Tom meant?"

15

Henry asked. "About the desert's being a dangerous place."

"It sounded like a warning to me," Violet said.

"What sounded like a warning?" Grandfather came out of the bathroom wearing his robe.

Jessie answered, "Tom Parker told us never to go out without water, that the desert is dangerous."

"He's right," Grandfather said. "The desert *is* dangerous if you're not prepared. Always carry a canteen, and wear a hat and sunscreen lotion. The sun is very hot."

"Hotter than Florida?" Violet asked, remembering the trip to Camp Coral.

"Much hotter. The desert is dry, so you must be careful not to become dehydrated." He yawned. "It's late. Gerald McCrae is picking me up early tomorrow. And you children have a lot of exploring to do."

After saying good night, the girls went into their tiny bedroom. Grandfather rolled the stepladder into position and climbed into the double bed built over the cab. Henry and Benny flipped the table against the wall and unfolded their bunks.

"I can see Mr. Tobias's trailer," said Benny, after the lights were out. "He's still up."

"Mmmm," Henry mumbled.

Benny was still wondering if they would have an adventure in Arizona when he fell asleep.

The next morning, a beat-up orange Jeep pulled up to the Aldens' RV.

Grandfather opened the door to greet a tanned, older man.

"I see my RV is still in one piece," the man said, his blue eyes teasing.

"Of course it's in one piece, Gerald," Grandfather said, laughing. "I had an excellent crew helping me." Then he turned to the children. "I'll be off now helping Mr. McCrae for the day. You kids have fun. See you later."

The Jeep pulled away in a swirl of gravel.

"Let's go eat breakfast!" Benny cried. "I'm starving!"

"So what else is new?" Jessie said, ruffling his hair.

They walked over to the Chuck Wagon. The restaurant was crowded.

Luis was already seated at a large, center table. He waved the Aldens over.

"My parents will be here later," he said. "They say they can't face food too early."

"It's never too early for me to face food!" Benny declared.

Janine brought them menus and a sloshing pitcher of water. The Aldens and Luis ordered bacon, eggs, toast, and juice all around.

"I see the Clarks over there," Jessie commented. "But not Mr. Tobias."

"Oh, he never comes in until dinnertime," Luis said.

"He stays up late," Benny put in. "I saw his lights on last night."

Luis nodded. "I sometimes see his lights on at dawn."

"Maybe he sleeps all day and stays up all night," Henry suggested.

Tom came in then, tipping his hat in greeting.

"Howdy, pardners!" he called when he saw the children.

"Howdy!" Benny called back. He liked talking cowboy lingo. "Thanks a heap, ma'am," he said to Janine, who brought their food, but Janine didn't even smile.

Violet watched the Clarks as she ate. Mrs. Clark was very pretty, with long, brown hair and a sparkling smile. Mr. Clark beckoned for Tom to sit with them. They seemed like a talkative couple.

"I bet they're on their honeymoon," Jessie said. "They look so happy."

"The Clarks *are* newlyweds," Luis said. "They're traveling all over the country in that fancy RV."

"I thought people who were just married didn't have very much money," Jessie said.

Just then the door opened, and a grizzled old man with a straggly gray beard stepped inside. He wore dirt-stained khaki pants and a sun-bleached denim shirt. A crumpled felt hat nearly hid his eyes.

"Boy, he's a real old cowboy," Benny said.

Luis lowered his voice. "That's Jake. He's a prospector. He lives up in the hills. He comes in here every morning for a cup of coffee and some supplies."

Henry noticed Tom Parker slip out the back door. Tom always seemed so friendly. Why didn't he greet Jake the way he did everyone else?

Janine spoke sharply to the prospector. "I'm not giving you any more credit, Jake. Pay up your bill."

"I'll pay you back with interest," said the old man. "I promise."

She snorted. "Your promises are like dust in the desert! I mean it, Jake. No food or supplies until you pay at least part of your bill."

"He doesn't have any money!" Violet said, concerned. "And he's hungry!"

Henry looked at Jessie. "What do you

think?" Since Grandfather was out all day, Henry and Jessie were in charge of the Aldens' money.

"Let's give him five dollars," Jessie said. She couldn't bear to see that old man go away hungry.

Henry went over to Jake. "I see you're a little short," he said, handing him a five-dollar bill.

"Many thanks," the old man said. "You won't be sorry. I'll pay you back soon. With interest!"

"What does he mean, 'with interest'?" Benny asked.

"It means he'll pay back our five dollars, plus some extra," Henry replied.

Janine took the money Jake paid her and stuffed it in her apron pocket. He shuffled back to the camping goods section.

"Next time, don't pay any attention to the old coot," she told the Aldens as she cleared their places. "He's got gold fever."

"What is gold fever?" Violet wondered when the woman left, clattering plates.

"Have you ever heard of the Lost Dutchman's mine in the Superstition Mountains?" Luis asked.

The Aldens shook their heads.

"Over a hundred years ago," Luis began, "a prospector claimed he found a fantastic gold mine somewhere in the Superstition Mountains. On his deathbed, he told his nurse how to find the mine. The nurse and two friends tried to locate the mine, but they never did. They told other people about the mine, and the story spread."

"And Jake is searching for the Lost Dutchman's mine?" Henry asked.

Just then Mr. and Mrs. Garcia came in. Overhearing Henry's question, they sat down and picked up the story.

"A lot of people have looked for the Dutchman's mine," said Mr. Garcia. "Jake is not alone. Gold fever is highly contagious. People get excited at the mention of gold."

Mrs. Garcia added, "People can look all they want, but no one can dig for gold in the Superstition Mountains. It's the law."

"Then why is old Jake still looking?" Jessie

asked. "If no one has found it in a hundred years, why does he believe *he* can find it?"

Mr. Garcia answered. "Not too long ago, some tourists found some small stone slabs with pictures carved on them. The stones were supposed to be maps, with clues to the location of the gold mine. If a person figured out the clues, they would find the mine. Like a treasure hunt."

"Where are the stones?" Benny asked. He liked the idea of a treasure hunt!

"They're in a museum in Mesa," said Luis. "I've seen them and have pictures of the stones in our RV."

"Can we see the pictures?" Henry asked eagerly.

"Sure."

"Luis, we'll be leaving on our hike after we eat," Mrs. Garcia told her son. "Would you like to come with us or stay with the Aldens?"

"I'd rather stay with my new friends." He looked eagerly at Henry. "If that's okay?"

"You bet," Henry said.

They all left the restaurant. Luis led the

way to his trailer and opened the door.

"Wow!" Benny commented when he stepped inside. "You sure have a lot of rocks!" Boxes overflowed with rocks in all shapes and sizes.

"I told you my parents are geologists. They can't resist picking up specimens." Luis took a folder from a drawer. "Here are the photographs of the stones."

Violet studied the pictures. Most of the stones were rectangular. One was heart-shaped. The heart-shaped stone fit into a heart-shaped hole in a larger stone.

"Why is this stone different from the others?" she asked.

"Some people think this stone points to Weaver's Needle," said Luis. "That's a landmark in the Superstition Mountains. It's one of the clues the prospector told his nurse, so everyone believes the mine is near the needle. If you look at Weaver's Needle a certain way, it looks like a half-buried heart."

"How can a needle look like a heart?" asked Benny.

Luis shrugged. "I don't think the rock

looks like either one. But the name stuck, I guess."

Henry noticed the stones were etched with squiggles and strange symbols. He squinted at some foreign words. "Do you know what that says?"

Luis grinned. "It's Spanish, which I happen to speak and read. It means, 'look for the heart' or 'follow the heart.' "

"Look for the heart," Jessie repeated thoughtfully.

"I have a question," Benny said. "Where *are* the Superstition Mountains?"

Luis spread his hand toward the brown hills behind the campground. "Right out there."

Henry felt a quiver of excitement. "We have pictures of the maps and Grandfather said we could explore. Why don't we look for the mine!"

"Yes!" agreed Benny eagerly. "We need a new adventure."

"Will you come with us, Luis?" Jessie asked. "After all, you have the map pictures."

"Well — " Luis hesitated. "I think it's too far for us to go without horses, but we could do some exploring in the area. Who knows what we might find."

"Yayyy!" Benny jumped up and down. "We're off again!"

"Let's get started," Henry said. "We'll go back to our trailer and get supplies."

Luis opened the door for them. As he did, a woman scurried away from the door.

It was Mrs. Clark.

She smiled guiltily. "Just hunting for my earring. I thought I lost one near here."

Violet stared at her. Mrs. Clark was wearing a lot of jewelry, including a gold chain and several chain bracelets. But no earrings.

Was the woman really looking for an earring? Or was she trying to listen to what they were saying about the lost mine?

CHAPTER 3

Benny's Gold

"Do you think we'll find the mine by lunchtime?" Benny asked Violet.

She clambered over a rock in the trail, then held out her hand for her brother.

"I doubt it, Benny," Violet said. "Luis said some people spend their whole lives looking for the mine."

Ahead on the trail, Luis stopped so the Aldens could catch their breath.

"It's best to go out in the desert early in the morning," he told them, "before the sun gets too hot. Drink water, even if you aren't thirsty. If you wait till you are, you're already becoming dehydrated."

The Aldens uncapped their canteens and took a long drink.

They all wore hats, sturdy shoes, and heavy socks. Luis had warned them that in the Superstition Mountains both plants and animals could sting or bite.

"Why is there a Superstition Mountain *in* the Superstition Mountains?" Jessie asked, confused.

Luis laughed. "Superstition Mountain is a special mountain in the Superstition Mountain range."

Henry gazed around the bare landscape. "It sure is different out here."

"But it's beautiful, too." Aiming her camera, Violet snapped pictures of a cactus that was as tall as a tree, with two arms reaching toward the sky.

"That's a saguaro cactus, right?" Henry remembered reading about them in Grandfather's Southwest guidebook.

Luis nodded. "They grow really slow, about two inches a year. It takes them fifty years to put out an arm."

"So this one must be at least a hundred years old." Jessie tipped her head back so she could see it better.

Luis squinted up at the sky. "We should probably head back. The sun is directly overhead. It's at its strongest."

"But we haven't found the mine yet!" Benny objected.

"Benny has gold fever," Henry teased. He scanned the horizon. "Anyway, we need to locate Weaver's Needle before we can begin searching for the mine. I wonder where it is."

"It's too far to walk to," Luis told him. "We'd have to ride horses."

Violet's eyes lit up. "Can we do that?"

"Grandfather told us we could rent horses," Henry said. "There's a stable just down the road from the campground."

Suddenly Benny leaped to his feet. "Gold!" He held a broken rock with a shiny gold lump sticking out. "I'm rich!"

Luis examined the rock. "It *looks* like gold, but it's really a mineral called pyrite. Sometimes it's called fool's gold, because people think they've found the real thing."

"It's pretty, though," Violet remarked.

With the hammer, Luis chipped away most of the broken rock. He handed Benny the stone. "Here you go. Now it's easier to carry."

Benny put his prize in his pocket. "I don't care if it's not real gold. I'm going to keep it forever. It will be my lucky rock."

Jessie was glad when they finally trudged back into camp. Their air-conditioned RV felt very nice. She made lemonade while the others cooled off.

No one had the energy to walk over to the Chuck Wagon for lunch, so they fixed a picnic of turkey sandwiches, chips, and chocolate cookies.

"You know what would feel great right now?" Henry said, fanning himself with a map of Arizona.

"A whole swimming pool of ice cubes?"

Benny guessed. His cheeks were still pink from the heat.

Henry laughed. "Close! A dip in a mountain lake."

Luis looked at the Aldens sprawled all over the furniture. "Well . . . the pool's open."

"The pool!" Jessie and Henry exclaimed at once.

Henry smacked his forehead. "We forgot all about the recreation center."

Benny was out the door in a flash.

After a reviving swim in the pool and three games of paddle tennis, the children collapsed in the lounge, which was furnished with comfortable leather chairs.

Benny pulled out his shiny rock and studied it in the slanting afternoon light.

Jessie hugged her knees. "Do you think there really is gold in the Superstition Mountains?" Jessie asked Luis.

"My parents laugh at the old legend," Luis replied, "but I think there is a lost treasure up there."

"Do you think *we* can find it?" Benny asked.

"Find what?" At that moment, Tom Parker came in, followed by Mr. and Mrs. Clark.

The Clarks were dressed for swimming. Tom was in his usual cowboy gear. He slouched on the sofa, propping his boots on the wagon wheel coffee table.

"Find what?" Tom asked again.

Henry shot Benny a warning glance. "Uh — we were wondering if we could find our way to the riding stables."

Tom gave him a quizzical look. "Well, it's as easy as finding the nose on your face. Just hike down the road a piece. Can't miss it."

"Oh, that sounds like fun!" Mrs. Clark squealed. "Can we rent horses and ride around here, Jim?"

Mr. Clark smiled at her. "But you don't ride."

"That's okay," Tom put in. "The animals at the stables are trail horses. Riding one of those gentle horses is like sitting in your living room."

Jessie was relieved. The Aldens hadn't ridden very much, either.

Luis stood up. "I guess my folks are back now. I'd better check in with them."

When he left, the Clarks settled into a couple of leather chairs. Mrs. Clark pointed to the rock Benny was polishing with the hem of his shirt.

"Looks like you struck gold, young man," she said.

"It's not *real* gold," Benny corrected. "I'm going to carry it in my pocket forever."

Tom leaned over to examine Benny's nugget more closely. "That's a mighty fine specimen. Where did you find it?"

Just then the door opened with a bang. Janine marched in. She looked angry.

"*There* you are." She glared accusingly at Tom. "You promised to unpack those boxes that were delivered this morning."

"So I did." Tom got up from the sofa. "By the way," he added to the Clarks, "my offer for an evening stroll in the desert still stands. Anytime you're ready, just holler."

He left, slamming the door. The Clarks

got up, too, and headed over to the pool.

Benny turned to Henry. "I wasn't going to tell anyone about the mine. I can keep a secret." He paused. "Except from Grandfather."

"Grandfather's okay," said Henry. "We can tell him. But nobody else."

Violet noticed something about Mrs. Clark. Earlier she had said she was looking for her earring outside the Garcias' trailer. At the time, she had on gold chains.

This afternoon, when she was going swimming, she wore a red stone pendant on a long silver chain, dangling earrings, and an armful of thin, silver bangles. She sure had a large selection of expensive jewelry.

Violet said to Jessie, "Isn't Mrs. Clark wearing a lot of jewelry to go swimming?"

Jessie nodded. "I was just thinking the same thing."

"I was wondering about Tom and Janine," said Henry. "She's always yelling at him to do some work."

"Don't mention the word 'work.' " Grandfather came in then, smiling.

Benny ran over to him. "You're back early today!"

"Yes, we're putting a new roof on his cabin, but it became too hot, so we knocked off early." He smiled at his grandchildren. "What have you been doing?"

They all spoke at once. Benny had to tell Grandfather about his fool's gold. Henry asked if they could rent horses tomorrow. Jessie told him about the sights of the desert. Violet mentioned she had taken some great pictures.

"Hold it! Hold it!" James Alden put his hand up. "How about dinner first, and then we'll discuss horses and fool's gold."

After a hearty supper of beef stew and cherry pie topped with ice cream, the Aldens went back to their RV.

"Do you believe there really is a lost mine?" Henry asked Grandfather. They had talked about the legend during dinner.

"That story has been around over a hundred years," Grandfather replied. "There must be some truth to it."

Violet was drawing the stone maps. She

had a good memory and remembered most of the details. "Then the mine is really out there?"

Grandfather patted her shoulder. "Gold makes people act strangely. People *want* to believe a fabulous gold mine exists."

Benny looked up at Grandfather. *He* believed the mine existed. And he wanted to find it.

"I want you all to have a good time in Arizona," Grandfather told them, "but please be careful."

It was bedtime. Everyone said good night.

In the little bedroom she shared with Violet, Jessie had trouble getting to sleep. Light was shining in her eyes.

She reached up to adjust the blinds. The light was coming from Mr. Tobias's trailer. Didn't that man ever go to bed?

Then Jessie saw something that made her heart skip a beat. A shadowy figure prowled around the Garcias' RV. The person seemed to be testing the window latches.

She was about to wake Violet when the figure melted into the desert darkness.

CHAPTER 4

A Warning!

The next morning, after Grand-father left early to help Mr. McCrae, the Aldens walked over to the Chuck Wagon. They shared a table in the corner with Luis.

Over a hearty rancher's breakfast of flap-jacks and sausage, they discussed the prowler Jessie had seen around the Garcias' RV.

"Maybe it was Mr. or Mrs. Garcia," Henry suggested.

Luis shook his head. "No, we were all in bed."

"Maybe it was Mr. Clark," said Violet.

"Or Mr. Tobias. He's always up late."

"But why would he be checking the windows in the Garcias' RV?" asked Jessie.

"Maybe," said Benny, "it was somebody else."

Henry looked at him. "Like who?"

"Somebody who isn't staying at this campground."

Jessie said, "RV Haven is several miles from the nearest town, right? There aren't any houses around. If the prowler isn't from the campground, then he — or she — would have to be from the mountains."

"Maybe Janine Crawford knows if anyone else lives around here," Henry said.

Janine hurried by just then with a pot of coffee.

"Excuse me, Janine." Henry used his politest tone. "Does anyone live out here? I mean, not on the campground."

"Nobody with a grain of sense," she snapped, slapping their check on the table. She left, her mood as sour as ever.

"Well, *that* was no help," Violet remarked.

Tom stopped by their table. "Going gold hunting today?"

"We're going *riding*," Henry replied cautiously.

Tom laughed, went over to the counter, and poured himself a cup of coffee.

"How did he know we're looking for the mine?" Henry asked Luis.

Luis shrugged. "It's kind of a joke around here. The mine is no secret. Remember, lots of people have looked."

Violet was quiet. She noticed that the Clarks, who sat across from them in a booth, kept getting up and passing their table. First Mr. Clark got up for a copy of the daily newspaper. Then Mrs. Clark walked by to get a bottle of catsup. Mr. Clark rose again to refill his coffee cup.

"Is it my imagination, or are the Clarks listening to us?" Violet said in a hushed voice.

"Violet's right," said Jessie. "They keep getting up and going right by our table. I think Tom Parker was listening, too, when we were talking about the prowler."

"Let's not mention the prowler to anyone," Henry advised. "Not until we find out more. Right now, everyone is a suspect."

Benny blissfully scooped up his last bite of hotcake. "Another mystery! We didn't have to find one — it found us!"

As they were making plans to rent trail horses, the door burst open.

Old Jake tottered into the restaurant. His battered felt hat was covered with dust. His clothes looked more rumpled than ever.

Jake glanced around, as if searching for a friendly face. His gray eyes rested on the Aldens. He headed in their direction.

"You loaned me some money," he said to Henry. "You seem like decent kids."

"Why don't you sit down?" Henry offered. Jake acted as though he had something important on his mind.

"Thankee." Jake pulled up an extra chair. He stuck out a calloused hand. "Name's Jake."

Henry shook his hand. "I'm Henry Alden. This is my sister Jessie, my sister Violet, and that's my brother, Benny. And our friend Luis Garcia."

Jake nodded at each in turn. "Nice to make your acquaintance." Suddenly lowering his voice, Jake asked, "Can you keep a secret?"

"Yeah!" Benny replied immediately. "What is it?" Old Jake must have found the Lost Dutchman's mine!

Jake pulled a crumpled piece of paper from his pocket. "When I got up this morning to start my campfire, I found this." He smoothed the paper on the table. Crudely cut-out letters spelled a single sentence.

Henry picked up the paper. "Looks like somebody wrote this using letters cut out of a flyer or something. But it's in Spanish. I can't read it."

"I can." Luis studied the note. "It says, 'This path is dangerous.' "

"What does that mean?" asked Violet.

"It means I'd better watch my back," Jake said, stuffing the note into his pocket.

"Who would send you that letter?" Luis wanted to know.

"Good question." Jake sighed. "When

you're a prospector, there's always somebody trying to jump your claim."

"Then you *have* found the mine!" Benny
exclaimed. "Where is it? We won't tell anyone, promise!"

But Jake clammed up. With a gruff
"Thanks for your help," he pushed back his
chair and hurried into the store section.

Janine followed Jake, grumbling, "Where
is Tom? He's never around when I have to
deal with difficult customers."

Suddenly Jessie thought of something.
"Jake!" she cried. "He lives in the hills.
Could he be the prowler I saw last night?"

"It's something to think about," Henry
said. "Jake is certainly a strange character."

The Garcias came in then.

"You early birds!" Mrs. Garcia teased as
Violet gave up her seat. "Please don't get
up."

"We were leaving anyway," Violet said.
"We're going horseback riding."

"Mr. Garcia, if someone *did* find the
Dutchman's mine, how would they say it
was theirs?" Henry asked.

"Well, you're supposed to file a claim with the local government," Mr. Garcia replied.

"But no one is permitted to stake a claim on federally protected land," added Luis's mother. "The Superstition Mountains are part of the Tonto National Forest. If anyone is digging in those hills, they are breaking the law."

Jessie and Henry looked at each other. Jake talked as if he had been digging in the hills. Was he in trouble with the law?

They discussed this as they hiked to the stables.

"Jake might not know he's breaking the law," Violet said. "Someone should tell him."

"He's been living in this area a long time," Henry said. "Seems like he would know."

"But what if he found the mine?" Benny asked. "Suppose he's already found the gold? Would he have to put it back?"

No one could answer that question. They were silent the rest of the way to the Mountain Shadows Stables.

A young man came out of the small office.

"I'm Rex. Looks like you youngsters aim to go riding."

"Yes, sir," replied Luis. "Do you have five saddle horses available?"

"Right this way." The man took them into the dim stables.

Violet loved the smell of hay and horses. She thought her horse was beautiful.

"What's his name?" she asked.

"Dusty," Rex replied. He brought out three horses for Luis, Jessie, and Henry. Then he led out a pony for Benny.

"This is Ginger," Rex told Benny. "If you give her a lump of sugar, she'll love you forever." He handed Benny a sugar cube.

Benny fed the sugar to Ginger. Her lips were soft and damp. "She tickles!" He giggled.

Then Rex saddled the horses and helped the children mount them.

Riding his cream-colored horse over the rocky ground, Henry felt like a cowboy from the Old West. "Which way is Weaver's Needle?" he asked Luis.

Luis studied the compass he had brought.

"That way," he said, pointing. "I don't know how far it is, though. Let's give it a try."

He led his horse to the beginning of the trail. The horses formed a single file with Luis at the head. Benny was next, followed by Jessie and Violet. Henry brought up the rear.

The trail wound upward between boulders and large cacti. The horses moved at a steady pace.

After they had been riding some time, Jessie turned around on her horse, Diamond, and grinned at Violet.

"Isn't this great?" she said.

At that moment, Luis cried out, "Benny!"

CHAPTER 5

Where Is Jake?

Jessie was riding right behind Benny. She, too, saw him lean over his pony's neck, then tumble off.

"Benny!" she exclaimed.

But Luis had already dismounted. "Are you okay?" he asked. Violet and Henry rushed up.

Benny brushed dirt off his shorts. "I'm okay." He grinned to show them he was fine.

"What happened?" Henry asked.

"I wanted to show Ginger my lucky rock,"

Benny explained. "Then she sort of twisted around, and I fell."

Luis stroked the pony's nose. "She probably thought you were feeding her a lump of sugar. Horses aren't very interested in lucky rocks."

Benny turned his pockets inside out. "My rock! Where is it?"

Violet picked up the shiny stone from the ground. "Here it is. You must have dropped it when you fell off." She handed it to him. "Put it in your shirt pocket, Benny, and fasten the button. It'll be safer there."

Jessie shaded her eyes from the glare of the sun. "What's that funny-shaped mountain up ahead?"

"That's Weaver's Needle," Luis replied.

Violet gasped. "It looks like a heart! Just like in the stone maps!"

"It does," agreed Henry. "Is that the 'heart' we're supposed to follow?"

"A lot of people believe so," Luis said, passing around his canteen.

Benny was excited. "What are we waiting for? Let's go!"

Luis shaded his eyes. "I don't know," he said thoughtfully. "The rock isn't as close as it seems."

"It's just over that hill," said Jessie.

"Distances are deceiving in the desert," Luis told her. "It's actually much farther away than it seems. And we'll have to hike the rest of the way, because the trail is too narrow for the horses."

"Do we have enough time today?" Henry asked.

Luis shook his head regretfully. "Sorry. We should have started earlier."

Violet was disappointed. "Will we ever start looking for the mine?"

"Tomorrow," Luis promised. "We'll get up early and be at the stables by six. We'll pack our breakfast and lunch."

Everyone agreed that they'd been out in the heat long enough. Remounting their horses, they headed back to the stables.

Halfway down the trail, they spotted a small dust cloud. Mr. and Mrs. Clark trotted up on matching horses.

Mr. Clark looked hot. He didn't even have

on a hat. Mrs. Clark was wearing shorts and tennis shoes. Neither of them was dressed for riding.

"Nice day for a horseback ride, isn't it?" Mrs. Clark said cheerfully. A diamond pin on her shirt flashed in the bright sun.

"Yes, but we're heading back," said Henry. "It's getting too hot."

"Is it?" said Mr. Clark. "I hadn't noticed." Sweat streamed down his red face. "Well, see you later."

They bumped down the trail.

Violet stared after them. "Did you see that fancy pin Mrs. Clark had on?" she said to Jessie.

"Just to go riding! There's something weird about those two," Jessie said.

When the Aldens and Luis returned to the stables, they asked Rex about the Clarks.

"Took my last saddle horses," Rex replied, shaking his head. "I told 'em they weren't properly geared for a midday ride, but they wouldn't listen. Said they knew what they were doing and paid me with a brand-new credit card."

"May we have these same horses tomorrow?" Luis asked Rex. "At six. Is that okay?"

"They'll be ready," Rex promised. "See you kids in the morning."

As they walked to RV Haven, they talked about the Clarks.

"Maybe they're looking for the mine, too," said Benny.

"If they are, they won't last long," Henry put in. "Mr. Clark wasn't even wearing a hat."

"Maybe Jake will find them," Violet said hopefully. "He could take them to his camp."

Luis was concerned, too. "If they aren't back by this evening, we ought to tell Tom and Janine. They might have to send out a search party."

"A search party!" cried Benny. "That's just like in the Wild West days."

Back at the campground, after everyone dressed in fresh clothes, they trooped into the Chuck Wagon for lunch.

"We ought to buy some supplies," Jessie said, while waiting for their sandwiches and soft drinks to arrive. "Especially since we're going to pack breakfast and lunch to-morrow."

As they ate, they discussed what they should take. Jessie and Henry planned a breakfast of fruit and granola. For lunch they would eat rolls, cheese, and cookies.

They strolled into the camp store. Benny picked out his favorite brand of cookies. Violet found some nice oranges. Henry bought an extra canteen.

Jessie took the supplies to the counter.

Janine rang up the purchases. "Nice that somebody actually pays their bill," she said when Jessie gave her the money.

Everyone knew she meant old Jake.

"Where is Jake?" Violet asked. "Has he been in yet today?"

"Haven't seen him," Janine replied.

Henry remembered what Luis had told him. "But Jake comes in every morning. Could something have happened to him?"

"Maybe he was tired today," Benny suggested.

"I'm worried," said Violet. "Jake looked

frightened yesterday when he showed us that note."

"Now we have three people to worry about," said Jessie. "First the Clarks, now Jake."

"We should wait until the end of the afternoon and then decide what to do," Luis said. "Let's go for a swim."

They spent an enjoyable afternoon at the recreation center. Between refreshing dips in the pool, they worked on a puzzle.

At around four o'clock, the Clarks straggled in. Mr. Clark's face was tomato red. Mrs. Clark looked wilted. Her ever present smile was gone.

"I told you to use sunscreen," she said to her husband. "Now you have a terrible sunburn."

"It's nothing," Mr. Clark snapped.

"Don't yell at me. We had to tell — " Mrs. Clark stopped suddenly, as if aware they weren't alone.

They passed the children with weak smiles.

"They're certainly acting strange," Henry

said. "I wonder why they went riding, since they obviously didn't enjoy it."

"At least we don't have to worry about the Clarks anymore," said Jessie.

Violet put her chin in her hands. "Now it's just Jake."

Just then Tom Parker came inside.

"Whoo-ee!" he exclaimed, wiping his face with an oversize red bandanna. "It's a scorcher out there today."

"Tom," Henry said. "Have you seen Jake today?"

Tom wrinkled his forehead. "Nope, don't believe I have."

"But he comes into the store every day," said Violet. "Do you suppose something has happened to him?"

Tom just laughed. "That old man is as tough as a gopher snake."

"Maybe so," Luis admitted. "But even gopher snakes get in trouble."

Tom narrowed his eyes in the afternoon light. He didn't look quite so friendly now, Violet thought.

"You kids shouldn't be fretting about an

old man. You're on vacation! Have fun!"

The Clarks made loud splashing sounds in the pool.

"Now, they've got the right idea," Tom said, jerking his thumb toward the pool room. "By the way, tomorrow evening is our desert hike. Don't forget!"

"Sounds great," said Henry. "Let's hope Jake is back by then so he can go with us."

"Don't concern yourselves with an old prospector." Tom's tone was light enough, but his eyes were still like slits.

When he left, Jessie spoke. "Something's fishy. Tom knows more about Jake than he's telling."

Henry nodded. "We have something more important to look for than the mine."

"Jake," said Benny.

That evening, Grandfather met them for dinner.

"The cabin is coming along nicely," he said, settling into their booth. "A few more days, and we'll be finished."

"In just a few days?" Violet said. That

didn't give them much time to find the mine — or Jake.

Grandfather asked the children what they had been doing.

"We rode horses into the hills," Benny said. "And I fell off Ginger, but I wasn't hurt."

Henry added, "We're taking a longer ride tomorrow. Don't worry, Benny will be careful. Won't you, Benny?"

"I'm always careful," Benny asserted. "It was Ginger who slipped, not me."

Grandfather listened to their plans, then nodded. "That sounds like fun."

It was late by the time they performed their evening chores. Soon everyone was ready for bed.

Benny shifted uneasily in his bunk. He hadn't been asleep very long. Something had awakened him. A sound?

He listened and heard nothing. That was it. The air-conditioning unit that ran constantly was silent.

Someone had shut off their air.

CHAPTER 6

Lights Out!

Benny sat up in bed. He listened carefully for the familiar sounds of the humming refrigerator and air conditioner. He heard only Grandfather's faint snoring.

A darting shape outside the window caught his attention. A tall, dark figure flitted between the Garcias' RV and Mr. Tobias's trailer.

"Henry!" Benny reached across and shook his brother.

Henry was awake in an instant. "What?"

"The air conditioner's not running," Benny said. "And I just saw somebody outside. Maybe it's the prowler Jessie saw the other night."

The air inside the RV was getting stuffy. Henry climbed out of his bunk and flicked on the light switch. The lights didn't turn on, either.

"The power's off," Henry reported. He climbed up to Grandfather's bed. "Grandfather, wake up. Something's happened to the power."

James Alden was up quickly. He began pulling his clothes on. The boys dressed hurriedly in the dark. By now the girls were awake, too.

"What is it?" Jessie called from the other end of the trailer. "How come the lights won't come on?"

"Something's wrong with the power," Grandfather said, grabbing his flashlight. "Henry and I will check it out."

"Me, too!" Benny scrambled after them.

Outside, all the RVs in the D Block were shrouded in darkness. Only small, overhead street lamps cast weak pools of light.

The door to the Garcias' trailer opened. Mr. Garcia and Luis stumbled down the steps. Mrs. Garcia followed them.

"Our power is out," said Mr. Garcia to Grandfather.

"Ours, too. Maybe a fuse in the main building blew," guessed James Alden.

"I'll go check with the management." Mr. Garcia headed toward the office. Mrs. Garcia went with him.

Luis came over to the Aldens' trailer. "I wonder what's wrong?" he asked.

Henry shone his flashlight around the hookup area. "Here's the problem," he said. "The cable's been disconnected." He held up the loose end of the plug.

Grandfather reconnected the cable. "That's strange."

Luis ran over to his RV's hookup. "Our plug has also been pulled! Yet the sewer and water pipes are still connected."

Inside the Aldens' RV, Violet tugged at

Jessie's sleeve. "Look," she said. "There are two people hanging around Mr. Tobias's trailer. Do you think we should warn him?"

"It's Mr. and Mrs. Clark," Jessie said, as the couple approached. She and Violet went outside. It was creepy inside the dark RV.

"Our electricity has been disconnected!" Mrs. Clark complained to Grandfather. "Yours, too? And the Garcias'?"

Mr. Clark was angry. "If this is somebody's idea of a prank, it's not funny. These trailers can get very hot."

"Fortunately, it's nighttime," said Grandfather. "The desert always cools down after dark."

Benny shivered and wondered if the prowler was watching them.

Henry and Luis refastened the cables to the Garciases' RV. Then they helped Mr. Clark fix his hookup.

Violet pointed to Mr. Tobias's RV. "What about Mr. Tobias? Should we check his hookup, too?"

Benny ran over. "It's okay," he called.

"That's funny," Jessie mused. "Everyone's

electricity was disconnected, *except* Mr. Tobias's."

"And he never even came out to see what was wrong." Henry stared at the metallic-colored trailer.

"Unless," Benny added, "*he* was the guy I saw running between the trailers."

This time Jessie shivered. "I sure hope we catch this prowler."

"Excitement's over," Grandfather said, herding them toward the RV. "Back to bed. We'll solve the mystery in the morning."

And if they didn't, thought Jessie, what would happen next?

Early the next morning, Gerald McCrae came by to pick up Grandfather. The Alden children rose early, too.

Jessie and Henry packed breakfast and lunch while Violet and Benny tidied the RV.

Luis knocked on the door.

"We're almost ready," Jessie told him. "Henry's filling the canteens now."

Luis looked pale in the faint morning light. "Someone got into our RV last night. The photographs of the stone maps were stolen!"

Henry turned from the sink. "Are you sure?"

"Yes. I knew we'd need them today. But when I opened the drawer, the folder was gone."

"Maybe your mother put it someplace else," Violet suggested.

Luis shook his head. "No. I'm certain the photographs were in the drawer last night."

"It must have happened when we were all outside!" Benny exclaimed.

"Benny could be right," said Henry. "The prowler could have sneaked into your trailer while everyone was fixing their electrical cables."

"We were all there," said Jessie. "Everyone except Mr. Tobias."

"What would Mr. Tobias do with my photographs?" Luis asked. "He hardly ever comes out of his trailer. We need those maps to find the exact location of Weaver's Needle."

"Wait!" Violet flipped open her drawing tablet. "I made some drawings of the stone

maps. They aren't perfect, but I have a pretty good memory."

Luis inspected her sketches. "Not bad. These seem fairly accurate. Nice work, Violet."

Pleased, Violet stashed her drawings into the backpack containing their food.

Henry strapped on the backpack and passed out the canteens. "If we hurry, we'll be at the stables by six."

Rex was waiting for them. Their horses had been saddled and fed. Each horse carried extra water rations.

"Have a good ride," Rex said, waving them off.

After a while they passed a sign that said "Peralta Canyon Trail."

"We're on the right track," Luis commented.

Once more they rode single file with Luis in the lead and Henry at the rear. They stopped once to eat their breakfast and again to drink and check their bearings.

"Are we almost there?" asked Benny.

Violet got out her maps. "I see Weaver's Needle," she said, pointing to the heart-shaped formation in the distance.

Luis nodded. "Soon we'll have to leave our horses and hike in."

After a while the trail ended, narrowing to a path that vanished in the brush. They tied the horses to the trees, and began climbing on foot.

"I keep thinking about old Jake out here. He must be really tough," Henry said.

"I hope he's all right," said Jessie.

Benny slowed his pace. "I don't see Weaver's Needle anymore," he said to Luis.

"That's because we're getting closer," Luis said.

Violet couldn't believe how quiet it was up here. Earlier the mountains echoed with birdcalls. Now the hills were completely silent.

Luis explained, "It's the heat. Animals and birds go under cover during the day. They come out to feed after sundown or in the early morning."

"I wish I could find some cover." Benny

slumped down on a stone. His cheeks were pink.

"Watch out!" Luis cried. He checked the boulder Benny sat on. "Always look before you sit down. A rattler could be sunning itself."

Benny jumped. "I sure don't want to sit on a snake!"

Henry had climbed over the next rise. "Hey, look what I found!"

The others hurried over the hill at the urgency in Henry's voice.

Henry stood in the middle of a small campsite. Charred sticks smoked from a recent fire. Paper cups and trash littered the area.

Violet picked up a coffee cup. "Is this Jake's camp? The fire is still warm. He's probably nearby."

Luis kicked at the smoldering ashes. "Jake is too smart to leave a mess like this. Anyone with wilderness experience would smother the fire with sand. And Jake would never leave trash."

"Then whose camp is it?" Benny asked.

"Somebody who obviously doesn't care." Henry was disgusted by all the trash lying around.

Jessie felt eyes boring into her. Looking up, she caught a glimpse of a tall figure in the rocks high above.

"Maybe it's *his* camp!"

Luis cupped his hands around his mouth. "Hey, up there!"

"Halloo!" Henry yelled. His voice bounced around the canyon.

But the figure disappeared into the rocks.

"Whoever it was," Benny said, "he didn't want to be found."

"We might as well eat," Jessie said. Henry shrugged off the backpack and Jessie began taking out rolls and cheese.

No one was very hungry. They were all disappointed they hadn't found Jake or his camp.

Violet couldn't stop thinking about the figure on the rocks. "That person we saw wasn't Jake," she said firmly.

"How do you know?" Henry asked, chewing a cookie.

"Because Jake isn't tall. And that person was tall."

"Like Tom," Jessie said thoughtfully.

"Or Mr. Clark," Luis added.

"Or," Henry said, "Mr. Tobias."

"Why would Mr. Tobias be out in these hills?" asked Violet. "He's always in his trailer."

Henry began picking up trash to stuff in his backpack. "Maybe he's not always in his trailer. Maybe he just wants us to *think* he is."

A pebble rolled down the rock wall. Henry froze. "He's still up there."

"What is he doing?" Jessie asked fearfully. "Why won't he answer us?"

"He's trying to scare us," Benny said.

"Well, it's working." Violet put her camera back in its case. She didn't feel like taking pictures.

"Violet's right," said Luis. "I think we should head back to camp."

"But we didn't find the mine," Benny cried.

"Or Jake," Violet said sadly.

CHAPTER 7

Lost!

"Tacos," declared Benny, "are the very best part of Arizona." He crunched his fourth beef taco happily.

"They *are* good," agreed Jessie, adding shredded lettuce to her chicken taco. "Mr. McCrae, it was really nice of you to take us out to dinner."

Across the table, Gerald McCrae chomped chips and salsa. "I couldn't think of a better way to celebrate finishing work on my cabin. James deserves a real Tex-Mex meal."

Grandfather refilled Violet's iced tea glass

from the frosty pitcher. "It felt good to work in the open air. And I'm so glad my grandchildren had a chance to see the West."

"Are we leaving?" Benny asked, concerned. They hadn't found Jake yet. Or really looked for the Lost Dutchman's mine.

"Not until the end of the week," Grandfather replied. "There are still a few things to be done on the cabin. Then Gerald will drive us to Phoenix and we'll fly home."

"And you'll take your RV to the cabin," Henry said to Mr. McCrae. "We've sure enjoyed it."

"I'll come visit you in Greenfield," said Mr. McCrae. "And you can borrow the RV again sometime."

Benny would miss the New Boxcar. It was neat living in that miniature house on wheels.

"How about fried ice cream for dessert?" Mr. McCrae suggested.

"How can they fry ice cream?" Benny wanted to know. "Wouldn't it melt?"

But when the toasted, coconut-covered ball was set in front of him, he didn't speak until the glass dish was scraped clean.

"Are you going on the evening hike with us?" Violet asked Grandfather as they drove back to RV Haven.

"Wouldn't miss it for the world," Grandfather replied. "The desert at night is beautiful."

The Aldens piled out of Mr. McCrae's Jeep in front of the Chuck Wagon.

"See you tomorrow morning," Gerald McCrae said to Grandfather, pulling away.

Grandfather went ahead to unlock the RV. "Since we're hiking in the desert, we'll all need warmer clothing," he told them.

Janine Crawford was closing the restaurant. The dinner shift was over.

"Did Jake come in today?" Jessie anxiously asked the waitress.

Janine jingled the large bunch of keys she carried. "I don't think so. To tell you the truth, I was too busy to notice."

"Wasn't Tom around to help?" Violet asked.

Janine made a snorting sound. "Is that man ever around when there's work to be done?"

"He's guiding the hike tonight, isn't he?"

Benny said. He didn't want to miss seeing the desert at night.

Janine got into her car. "Don't worry. If it's something fun, Tom will be there."

"She doesn't like him very much, does she?" Henry observed as Janine's car pulled away, crunching gravel.

Violet noticed something about the waitress. "Janine is tall," she said. "As tall as any man. Do you suppose she was the person we saw on the rocks today?"

Henry nodded. "Good point, Violet. We can't say for sure if the prowler or the stranger in the hills was a man."

"All I know," Benny said, "is that Jake hasn't shown up in two whole days."

"Sounds to me like the threat in Jake's note came true. I think Jake's in trouble," Jessie said.

Back in the RV, the children got ready for the hike. Jessie and Violet tied sweaters around their waists. Henry and Benny changed into long-sleeved shirts. Since Benny's shirt didn't have a pocket on the front, he tucked his lucky rock into his jeans pocket.

They all gathered at the recreation center. The Clarks and the Garcias were already waiting, along with several other people from the campground. Luis joined the Aldens.

Tom Parker strode into the lounge area. He wore soft, knee-high boots and a long, suede duster with fringed sleeves. His silver belt buckle sported a large turquoise stone that matched the stone in his string tie. His cowboy hat was black, with a jaunty white feather.

"Wow," breathed Benny. He gazed longingly at Tom's boots. More than ever, he wished he were a cowboy.

"Don't you look handsome," Mrs. Clark teased. "Like a real guide from the Old West."

Tom tipped his hat gallantly. "Thank you, ma'am. All right, pardners! Let's hit the trail!"

The group moved outside to the western end of the campground. From the pavement they struck off on a path bordered with white pebbles.

Violet held Grandfather's hand. "Look at

the sunset," she said. "I count five shades of purple."

"It is spectacular," Grandfather agreed.

She looked back once, at the trailers and RVs bathed in lavender light. She saw a pale, ghostly face in the window of the silver Airstream.

It was Mr. Tobias. He wouldn't even leave his trailer to go on a hike. He didn't seem to like people at all. Why was he so unsociable?

As the sun disappeared over the horizon, Tom talked about the desert.

"As soon as the sun goes down," he said in a lecturing tone, "small animals come out to feed. It's too hot during the day, so kangaroo rats and mice sleep. But when they come out, so do their enemies."

Jessie slipped her arms into her sweater. "What kind of enemies?" she asked him.

"Foxes," he replied. "Coyotes. Scorpions and gila monsters."

"Monsters? There are monsters out here?" Benny reached into his pocket and touched his lucky rock.

Luis reassured him. "A gila monster is a

large lizard. Don't worry. It moves very slowly. And it eats insects."

Mr. Clark asked Tom a question about the various cacti growing beside the trail.

"The saguaro cactus lives to be hundreds of years old," Tom said knowledgeably. "It grows a branch every twenty years."

"Twenty years!" Mrs. Clark was impressed.

Henry exchanged a look with Luis. "Didn't you tell us the saguaro grows an arm every *fifty* years?"

Luis nodded. "I hate to say it, but Tom is wrong."

Jessie was wondering why Tom sounded as if he was reading from a textbook. He had dropped his easygoing speech and his tone was stiff.

It was nearly dark when the group stopped at a circle of large, flat stones. In the center was a small, charred pit.

"Gather brush," Tom ordered everyone. "Soon we'll have a roaring fire. Then I'll tell you some tall tales."

Benny was proud to gather the most

brush. "Are you going to start a fire with two sticks?" he asked Tom eagerly.

Tom knelt over the pit. "Takes too long, Benny," he said. "Besides, there's no sun to create a spark." With a lighter, he nervously flicked at the brushpile again and again.

The fire would not catch.

"Can I try?" offered Mr. Garcia. "I've had a lot of experience with balky campfires."

"So have I!" Tom barked. "I've lived in Arizona all my life — I know how to start a fire."

Mr. Garcia backed away, taking a seat next to his wife.

Finally a flame licked over the brush. "Sorry," Tom said to Mr. Garcia. "I guess the wind wasn't right."

"There is no wind," Violet whispered to Henry as they all found a seat around the fire.

"I know," Henry said. "It's perfectly still tonight."

Tom was definitely acting strangely.

"How about a story?" asked one of the other campers.

"Do you know one?" Tom joked. But he seemed distracted, as if he couldn't think of a story of tell.

Benny raised his hand and waved it. "Tom, tell us about the Lost Dutchman's mine." That was a story they would all enjoy.

In the leaping firelight, Tom's face twisted. "I don't know that story, Benny. Maybe you could share it with us."

Jessie's jaw dropped. A native Arizonan like Tom didn't know the legend of the Lost Dutchman's mine?

Grandfather came to the rescue. He told a long, funny tale that made everyone laugh.

Benny was tired from that morning's long ride in the hills. He leaned against Jessie's shoulder and dozed off.

Henry, who was sitting next to Violet, gently nudged her.

"Look out there," he whispered. "Do you see anything strange?"

Violet stared beyond the fire. The last light of the day silhouetted cacti and rocks

on the ridge. Then she saw it, an armless saguaro. Or was it a man?

"That cactus," she whispered back. "It looks like a person!"

"I wonder if it's the prowler," Henry said. "Watching us. Two of our suspects are right here, Mr. Clark and Tom. That leaves Mr. Tobias."

"And Janine," Violet said, reminding him the mysterious stranger could be a woman. "Maybe it's just a person-shaped cactus."

"You could be right. The night plays tricks on our eyes." But the more Henry stared at the "cactus," the more he was certain it was human.

Across the circle, Mr. Clark let out a big yawn. "Well, I think it's about time to head on back to the bunkhouse."

"I agree," said Grandfather. "We all have another busy day tomorrow."

Very busy, thought Jessie. Time was running out. They would have to find Jake.

Mrs. Clark came over. "Oh, your little brother fell asleep. He's so cute. Here, let me help you with him."

"That's okay," Jessie said, shaking Benny awake. "We're fine."

But Mrs. Clark insisted on taking Benny's arm and helping him to his feet.

After a while, the cool desert air woke Benny up completely. He reached into his pocket to touch his lucky rock.

The pocket was empty.

"My rock!" he exclaimed. "I can't find it!"

"Not your lucky rock?" Jessie cried. "Oh, Benny!"

Benny turned all his pockets inside out. "It's missing!"

"You mean that shiny rock?" said Mrs. Clark. "Oh, it's probably back at the trailer. Or the restaurant. You could have left it anywhere."

"No, I didn't," Benny insisted. "I put it in my pocket before we left for the hike. And now it's gone!"

It was too dark to search the area. Grandfather and the others were waiting for him.

Benny slipped his hand nervously into Jessie's. He didn't trust Mrs. Clark.

When he first showed her his gold rock,

she had eyed it enviously. It was obvious she liked pretty things from all the shiny jewelry she wore.

Could Mrs. Clark have stolen his lucky rock?

CHAPTER 8

The Storm

"One more day," Grandfather announced at breakfast the next morning. "Gerald and I have only one more day of work, then his cabin will be finished. We'll spend tomorrow relaxing, and then we'll head back home Saturday."

Henry and Jessie looked at each other. One more day. That's all they had to find Jake.

A beep outside indicated Gerald was there to pick up Grandfather. He left in the battered orange Jeep.

The restaurant wasn't very busy this

morning. Mr. Tobias was never at breakfast, and the Clarks, sitting at their regular table, seemed unusually quiet. Jessie noticed that Mrs. Clark wasn't wearing any of her flashy jewelry. Mr. Clark looked as if he hadn't slept.

Even more odd, Tom didn't come in to greet the guests.

"He'd better be fixing the pool filter," Janine said, when Henry asked about Tom. "I've been after him over a week."

Luis breezed in. "Has Jake been in yet?" he asked anxiously.

Violet shook her head. "We haven't seen him."

Jessie told Luis that they were only staying until Saturday.

"We want to look for Jake," Henry added. "We're afraid something has happened to him, especially since he got that threatening note."

Luis agreed. "It's still pretty early. I'm sure our horses will be available."

They split up to pack food and water for the expedition.

At Mountain Shadows Stables, Rex seemed glad to see them.

"Benny," he said, "Ginger has been pining away for you. Now she'll perk up."

In no time he had the horses saddled and ready to go.

"Here, Ginger," Benny crooned to the pony. "I brought you some sugar." He felt in his pocket for the sugar cube he saved from breakfast. His fingers missed the warm, familiar shape of his lucky rock.

Violet sensed her brother's sadness. "Maybe you'll find another rock like the one you lost," she said.

"Maybe." Benny knew they wouldn't have much time to search for lucky rocks, not if they had to look for Jake.

They followed the Peralta Canyon Trail. When the trail ended, they left their horses securely tied and watered them.

"Let's try another way to Weaver's Needle," Luis said, referring to Violet's map drawings. "Maybe this time we'll find Jake's camp."

It was a long, hot climb. The Aldens and

Luis stopped often to gulp from their canteens.

Benny scampered ahead of the others. He had a strong feeling there was something important just beyond that next group of boulders.

Suddenly Benny shrieked. "Hey, I found it!"

Jessie looked back at Violet. "Do you think he's found the mine?"

"Knowing Benny," said Violet, "a lost mine wouldn't stay lost for long."

But they were wrong.

Just beyond an outcropping of rock, a campsite was nestled in a small canyon. A sleeping bag lay unrolled in the dirt. Pans and a tin coffeepot were scattered about.

Luis hopped down from the rock and looked around.

"I bet this is Jake's camp," he said. "This is a good location — not too far from Weaver's Needle, yet hidden."

"I'm surprised Jake would leave such a mess," Violet said.

"He didn't." Henry plucked a scrap of fabric from the edge of a rock. "See this? It matches the sleeping bag. I bet Jake tucks his bedroll behind this rock."

Luis nodded. "To protect it from the weather. You're right, Henry. And this flat rock could be where he stores his supplies."

"There," Benny pointed to the ground. Nearly hidden by a rock was Jake's old felt hat.

"Either Jake left in a big hurry," Jessie mused, "or somebody wrecked his camp. On purpose."

Henry felt the ashes of an old fire. "Cold," he said. "If it's Jake's camp, he hasn't built a fire in a while." He pointed to the ground. "See these footprints? They were made by a man a lot bigger than Jake."

Violet examined the dust-filled outlines. "They look like they were made by someone with new boots. See how sharp the lines are? Jake's boots were old and worn. I'll bet these prints were made by the person who ruined Jake's camp."

"Maybe that person is here right now," Benny said in a hushed tone. "Hiding from us."

The thought of the boot-heeled stranger watching them made Jessie nervous. "Do you suppose this person did something to Jake?"

"I think we should go back to the campground and call the authorities," Henry said decisively. "Jake could be seriously hurt."

They all agreed this was the right thing to do. After hiking back to their horses, they rode to the stables.

"Come back real soon," Rex said as they left Mountain Shadows.

When they got back to the trailer park, a strong wind began to gust, kicking up swirls of dust.

"Ow!" cried Benny, shielding his bare legs with his hands. "That sand stings!"

They headed for the restaurant. Janine Crawford rushed out, her dark brows drawn together in fury.

"Skipped out!" she exclaimed. "Skipped out without paying their bill!"

"Who?" asked Henry.

"The Clarks, that's who!" Janine gestured in the direction of Block D. Sure enough, the fancy RV was missing. "Owed four weeks of hookup plus a huge bill for food!"

"Did they go up into the mountains?" Violet asked. Maybe the fresh bootprint belonged to Mr. Clark.

"How should I know?" Janine said. "And do you think Tom was around to warn me they were skipping out?"

"Tom's missing, too?" Jessie wondered if Tom left with the Clarks.

Janine went back into the restaurant, still ranting.

Luis stared at the Aldens. "This is weird. The Clarks, Tom, *and* Jake are all missing. And nobody knows anything!"

Henry gazed at the silver Airstream. "Maybe somebody does. Let's go ask Mr. Tobias if he saw the Clarks leave."

But when he knocked on the trailer door, there was no reply.

"Mr. Tobias?" Benny called. "Are you in there?"

Still no response.

"He must be in there," Luis said. "He never goes anywhere. And his car is still attached to the trailer."

"I guess he's asleep," Violet suggested. She turned her head as the wind whipped dust into her face. "Look!"

A shiny black car pulled up to the main office. A man in a white shirt and striped tie got out and strode to the door. When he saw the office was empty, he walked over to the restaurant.

The Aldens went inside the restaurant, where the man was questioning Janine.

"I told you, I don't know where they are," Janine insisted, furiously wiping the counter with a rag. "If I did, I'd have the law on them. They could be anywhere."

"Well, you won't mind if I look around the campground," the man told her.

"Suit yourself."

Outside, the man stalked around the

campground, peering into trailer windows.

"He's sure suspicious," Benny said. "Does he think the Clarks are hiding in another trailer?"

"I wonder why he wants Mr. and Mrs. Clark," Jessie said.

"Let's look for Tom," Henry said. "Maybe he knows what's going on around this camp."

Luis pointed to a low building behind the recreation center. "That's the bunkhouse. Maybe he's in his room."

The wind storm grew worse as they crossed the parking lot. The door to the bunkhouse banged open and shut like a broken shutter.

"I guess Tom forgot to lock the door this morning," Henry said. Cupping his hands around his mouth, he yelled, "Tom! Are you in there?"

The wind was so strong, his words could barely be heard. Tumbleweeds rolled across the parking lot.

Litter and food wrappers flew out of the bunkhouse door. Inside, they could see socks, boots, and newspapers scattered on the floor.

"Guess Tom isn't very neat," Benny observed.

"That looks like a Spanish-English dictionary," Luis said, pointing to a small book lying near the doorway.

The wind kicked up another strong gust. Benny stooped to pull off a sheet of paper that had plastered itself to his leg. He stared at the paper, his mouth in an "o."

"What is it?" Henry said.

Benny held up the paper so they could all see the holes slashed in it. The sheet was an advertisement, with letters roughly cut out.

Violet gasped. "This must be where Jake's threatening note came from!"

"And he used the dictionary to translate his message into Spanish," Jessie added. "Why would Tom Parker send old Jake a warning note?"

Other papers fluttered from the open doorway. Before the wind snatched it away, Jessie planted her foot on a photograph.

"Luis! Isn't this one of your maps?"

Luis grabbed two more escaping sheets. "So are these! What were my map pictures doing in Tom's room?"

Violet trapped a piece of wind-blown paper against the wall. She flattened the sheet with the palm of her hand, then studied the paper.

"I think this will answer a lot of questions," she said.

CHAPTER 9

One Mystery Solved

The others gathered around Violet.

"It's a letter from Tom," she said. "It's to somebody named Frank. See? It's signed 'Tom Parker.' "

Violet squinted at the messy handwriting. " 'My great-uncle Jake,' " she began, then gasped. " 'My great-uncle Jake, the prospector, has no idea who I am . . . can't wait to get my hands on his mine. Then I'll have a new address — Easy Street.' "

Her eyes huge, she glanced up from the

page. "Tom is Jake's great-nephew. And Jake doesn't know it!"

"Where's Easy Street?" Benny asked. "Maybe that's where Tom is now."

"It's an expression," Jessie answered. "It means he'll have plenty of money."

"This sounds like trouble," Henry said. "First we find that advertisement with the letters cut out — "

" — just like Jake's warning note," Luis broke in. "And now this letter." His tone became serious. "If Tom wants Jake's mine, then that means Jake has found the Lost Dutchman's mine!"

"But where is Jake?" Jessie asked. "Did Tom go to his great-uncle's camp? Was he the man who left the footprints — and the man we saw on the rocks — " Her words trailed off. She was really afraid something bad had happened to Jake.

"We need to find Tom," Henry said firmly. "Tom is the key."

"He's sure not here," Benny said, peering into the deserted bunkhouse. "Let's go back to the restaurant and see if he's there. Besides," he added, "I could use a piece of apple pie right about now."

Despite their worries, the others laughed. No matter what the crisis, Benny was always hungry!

They didn't find Tom in the restaurant. But the stranger who had driven up in the shiny black car sat perched on a stool. His white shirt was stuck to his back with sweat and his striped tie was flopped over one shoulder. He guzzled a large iced tea.

When he saw the Aldens and Luis, he swiveled around.

"Just the people I want to talk to," he said. "You're the Aldens from Two-D, correct?"

Henry answered, "That's right."

"Do you know anything about your neighbors taking off? You know, the Clarks, in that big RV?"

Jessie shook her head. "No, sir. We saw them this morning at breakfast, but then we went riding. When we came back, they had already left."

The man sighed. "It's the same old story."

"What story? How come you're looking

for Mr. and Mrs. Clark?" Benny asked. "Are you a relative?"

"No, I represent a bank. The Clarks borrowed money from our bank to buy that motor home." He frowned. "They never made any payments on their loan. They kept moving from state to state. So the bank sent me to track them down and take back the motor home."

Benny hopped up on the stool next to the man. "It doesn't sound like a very fun job."

The man smiled wanly. "It's not. But people like the Clarks make jobs like mine necessary. They also bought a lot of expensive jewelry on credit that they've never paid for, either."

"I didn't think newlyweds were supposed to have much money," Jessie said.

"They don't, usually," the man said. "Most couples save until they can afford luxuries. The Clarks didn't want to wait. They made a habit of buying things they couldn't afford and then skipping out."

"They seemed like such nice, happy people," Violet said wistfully, remembering Mrs. Clark's smile.

"They won't be so happy when I catch up to them," the man said. "And I *will* find them. A motor home like theirs isn't easy to hide. I'll stay on their trail."

The man left then, after wishing them all a good day.

"I can't believe people buy things and never intend to pay for them," Jessie said, indignant. She wondered if Tom Parker had skipped town with the Clarks. He fit into the puzzle somewhere.

"People do it all the time," Janine remarked, dropping the man's change in the cash register drawer. "Just like old Jake."

"But Jake says he'll pay you back," Benny insisted. "With interest. That's what he says."

"Yes, he does." Janine softened a moment. "I wonder where the old guy is? He hasn't been in here for a cup of coffee in days."

"That's what we want to — " Henry began, then stopped as the cowbell on the door jangled.

Mr. Tobias came inside. He wore a wrinkled white T-shirt and jeans. Under his eyes were blue smudges, as if he hadn't slept in a long time.

"Coffee, Janine," he said to the waitress. "Make it extra strong, please."

He chose a stool at the counter, then looked at the Aldens, who stared back at him.

"Mr. Tobias," Violet stated. She recognized the pale face she had seen in the window of the silver trailer as they left for the desert hike last night.

"Yes, I am," Mr. Tobias answered. "Can I do something for you, young lady?"

"Do you know where Jake is?" she asked at last.

Mr. Tobias sipped his coffee. "Who? I don't know any Jake."

"He's the old prospector," Henry said. "He comes in here to buy groceries. He's looking for the Lost Dutchman's mine. And Tom Parker is his nephew."

"Great-nephew," Jessie corrected. "But Jake doesn't know this."

Mr. Tobias furrowed his brow. "Wait a minute. You kids are going too fast for me. Tom Parker is related to this Jake character?"

"Yes," Luis spoke up. "And we think Tom wants to get Jake's mine. Maybe he did something to his great-uncle. They've both disappeared."

"Well, if Jake is a prospector, he'll be just fine," Mr. Tobias speculated. "But that Tom Parker won't last five minutes if he's lost in the hills."

"Why?" asked Benny. "Tom's a real cowboy."

Mr. Tobias laughed so hard, his coffee spluttered. "Tom Parker a real cowboy! What a joke! The man is no more a westerner than I am."

"But those outfits he wears . . . and the way he talks," Jessie said. But then she remembered how Tom's desert lecture sounded as if he was reading from a textbook.

"Fake. Everything Tom Parker knows

about the West he read in books. And you can buy those clothes in Phoenix," said Mr. Tobias.

"How do you know this?" Henry asked suspiciously.

"For one thing, his clothes are too new-looking. Real cowboys look rugged, like they've been riding the trail. And real cowboys don't go around calling everybody 'pardner.' Tom must get his lingo from old westerns."

"He tricked us!" Benny exclaimed.

Janine set the coffeepot down with a thump. "He fooled me, too. That slick talker! No wonder he couldn't fix the filter on the pool or take care of the grounds around here. He probably doesn't know how."

"Where is he now?" Henry asked, going to the window.

Outside the raging wind chased debris across the parking lot.

Luis joined him. "We're in for a real dust storm. If anybody's out in that, they'd better take cover."

"I hope poor Jake is okay," said Jessie.

"Tom is probably miles away with the Clarks."

At that moment, the door burst open in a gust of stinging sand. Two figures stumbled in, one shoving the other ahead of him.

"Any coffee on?" said a familiar voice. "I sure could use a cup."

Benny launched himself off the stool. "Jake!" he cried. "Where have you been?"

"Out hunting," said the old man, flapping his dust-covered hat. He pushed a surly-looking Tom Parker into the nearest booth. "Look at the varmint I caught." Jake laughed hoarsely.

Tom scowled at the floor. His jeans were filthy and his silver-studded cowboy shirt was ripped. His hat was nearly as battered as Jake's old felt hat.

"What's going on?" Janine demanded. "Jake, is it true Tom is your great-nephew?"

The old man snorted. "Yes, I suppose he truly is related, though I'm ashamed to claim him."

"What happened?" Henry asked. "How do you know this?"

"Well, you saw that note I got a few days ago. Then I noticed somebody had been nosing around my camp." Jake gratefully accepted the mug of coffee Janine handed him. "So I set a trap for him."

"Like a mousetrap?" Benny asked.

Jake smiled through his brushy mustache. "I hid out for a couple of days, waiting to see if he'd come back. Sure enough, he did. Then I caught him."

Jake went on. "Turns out Tom has a bad case of gold fever. He thought he would waltz in and take my claim, after all my hard work."

"Tom said he wanted to live on Easy Street," Benny put in.

Jake threw back his head in laughter. "Guess I showed him!"

The Aldens were full of questions.

"Did you break into Luis's RV?" Benny asked Tom.

"The door was open," Tom said.

"You stole the pictures of the stone maps," Henry accused. "And you cut off our electricity to get us all outside."

"And left a messy camp in the mountains," Benny added.

Tom didn't deny it. "Mrs. Clark told me about the map pictures. She heard the Garcia kid talking to you about it and she knew I was looking for the Dutchman's mine."

"Did you know the Clarks are gone?" Jessie asked.

"Who do you think tipped them off about the man from the bank?" Tom smiled thinly. "The Clarks and I had a deal. I'd keep their little secret and they'd help me."

"How did you know the Clarks were in trouble with the bank?" Mr. Tobias asked.

"I checked them in the day they came. Thought something was funny about them. Mrs. Clark had a wallet full of brand-new credit cards." Tom laughed. "What they say about crooks is true. It takes one to know one."

"So you became friends," Henry said.

"Let's just say we were useful to each other," Tom replied. "The Clarks brought supplies to my camp, little things like that. In town yesterday I saw the man from the bank asking about a couple with a fancy trailer. I knew he'd pay RV Haven a visit, so I warned the Clarks."

Janine pointed her finger at Tom. "I don't know what else you've done, but you're through at RV Haven. Pack your things and be gone by nightfall."

"Don't worry. I'll be glad to get back to civilization." Tom stalked out the door without a backward glance.

"Good for you," Jake said to Janine.

The waitress smiled. "How about some apple pie à la mode? On the house?"

"For me?" Jake seemed touched by her gesture.

"For everyone!" Janine said generously.

"Yay!" cried Benny. Apple pie was exactly what he needed.

CHAPTER 10

Benny's Surprise

The Chuck Wagon looked especially festive that night. Country music played from the jukebox. Orange and yellow streamers looped the counter. A pink and green piñata in the shape of a bull hung from the ceiling.

"Wow!" said Benny. "Who did all this?"

Jake came out from the kitchen, wiping his hands on a towel. "I did. How do you like it?"

"It's different," Violet remarked.

Jake himself looked different. He had

shaved off his scraggly beard. His mustache had been neatly trimmed and he wore clean khaki pants and a denim shirt.

"Grandfather, can we sit at that large table? The Garcias are eating with us," Jessie said.

"You bet," Grandfather replied.

Jake ushered the Aldens to the round center table and handed out menus with a flourish.

"Where's Janine?" asked Violet. She didn't see the dark-haired waitress at her usual station by the cash register.

"She'll be along," Jake said mysteriously. "Meanwhile, I'll take your drink orders."

Benny and Violet ordered soft drinks, while Henry, Jessie, and Grandfather opted for iced tea with lemon.

The Garcia family came in and joined the Aldens.

"Tomorrow is your last day here," said Mrs. Garcia. "I hope you have enjoyed your stay in Arizona."

"And how!" Benny declared.

"I took some great pictures," said Violet. "We'll never forget this trip."

Henry and Luis exchanged addresses so they could write to each other.

Jessie sat back in her chair. It felt good to relax with friends, but there were still many unanswered questions. Why did Mr. Tobias hide in his trailer? And why was Jake working in the restaurant?

The bell jangled and Mr. Tobias came in.

James Alden waved his arm. "Come join us," he offered.

Mr. Tobias gave a small smile. "I'd be delighted. After a long day at the typewriter, I could use the company."

"Are you working on another novel?" Grandfather asked.

Henry stared at Grandfather. "Novel? Do you know Mr. Tobias?"

Grandfather laughed. "I know his work. He's a fine mystery novelist." He spoke to Mr. Tobias. "I recognized you from the jacket photo of your last book. I assumed you were hard at work on a new mystery."

"You deduced correctly," Mr. Tobias said, chuckling. "That's why I came out here. So I could work in private."

Benny was surprised. "You write mystery books? Boy, you should write down some of our stories. We solve mysteries all the time."

"All except this one," said Jessie dolefully. "We don't have all the answers."

Janine breezed into the restaurant. Her normally sour face was lit with a smile. She was actually perky.

"Nice going!" she praised Jake as she took in the decorations. "You really spiffed up the place."

Jake brought a tray of iced tea to the Garcias and Mr. Tobias. "I found a box of party stuff in the back. Glad you like them."

"You'll work out okay," Janine praised Jake, tying on her apron.

The Aldens and Luis were completely mystified.

"Will somebody tell us what's going on?" Henry demanded.

Janine laughed. "Meet my new coworker."

Jake bowed modestly. "Miss Janine and I

are in the dining business together."

"I hired Jake to take Tom's place," Janine explained. She seemed much happier. "Already Jake is a thousand times better than that lazy Tom Parker."

The Aldens had filled Grandfather in on Tom Parker's activities.

"I still can't believe that young man did all those things," Grandfather said now. "Wrote threatening notes, lied about his background, stole Luis's maps." He shook his head in disbelief.

"I had my eye on him," Jake said, bringing baskets of warm tortilla chips and dishes of salsa. "He always ducked out whenever I came into the store."

"I noticed that." Henry dunked a chip into the peppery sauce. "Was that you watching us the night Tom took us on the desert hike?"

Jake nodded. "I knew something was funny about that guy. Then I saw him try to build that fire!" He hooted.

"He wouldn't let anyone help," added Mr. Garcia.

"And he disconnected our electrical cables

so he could get into our trailer," said Mrs. Garcia in disbelief.

Mr. Tobias spoke up. "I heard someone outside my trailer that night. I went to the door and whoever it was ran away. I guess I scared him away."

"Then why didn't you tell us?" Jessie said.

The writer smiled sheepishly. "To be honest, I was working on a crucial part of my story. I couldn't leave my typewriter until I had written that chapter. After that, I just forgot about it."

Grandfather nodded. "I've heard writers can be that way. They just block out the whole world."

Benny swung his feet idly. The biggest, most important mystery hadn't been solved. When Jake came back with a tray loaded with enchiladas, tamales, jalapeño cornbread, refried beans, and tacos, Benny saw his chance.

"Jake," he said loudly, "did you find the Lost Dutchman's mine?"

A dull flush crept up Jake's clean-shaven cheeks.

"Benny," admonished Violet. "That's Jake's business, not ours."

"Well, actually, it's the state's business," Mr. Garcia said. "It's against the law to dig in the Superstition Mountains."

Jake glanced around the restaurant. Janine was busy in the back. There were no other customers besides Mr. Tobias, the Garcias, and the Aldens.

Putting his finger to his lips, he pulled a paper out of his pocket. He handed the old, yellowed paper to Mrs. Garcia.

She read the document silently, then handed it to her husband, who also read it. Mr. Garcia folded the paper carefully and passed it back to Jake.

"All is in order," Mr. Garcia said.

Benny was bursting with curiosity. "What did the paper say?"

Mrs. Garcia grinned at him. "It said that Jake staked a claim before the law went into effect. He is excused from that law. Legally, he is permitted to dig."

"You found the mine?" Benny's eyes were like saucers.

Jake's smile was secretive. "Let's just say I found . . . something."

Benny stared at the prospector, awestruck. For once, he was not first to reach for the taco plate.

Dinner conversation drifted away from lost gold mines. The Garcias talked about their work as geologists. Mr. Tobias spoke about writing mysteries. He could only write at night and sleep during the day, which explained his odd hours.

Grandfather had finished helping Gerald McCrae with his cabin. Tomorrow was the Aldens' last day at RV Haven.

"What would you like to do?" Grandfather asked.

The Alden children had different ideas.

"Go riding," Violet suggested. She would like another ride on her horse, Dusty.

"Hang around the pool," Jessie said.

"Hike into the mountains one last time," Henry put in.

"All of those ideas sound fine," Grandfather said approvingly. "No reason why we can't do them all." He turned to his youngest grandchild. "What about you, Benny? What would you like to do?"

"I bet I know," Luis said with a grin. "Go look for the Lost Dutchman's mine. Am I right, Benny?"

"Well . . . you know what I'd really like to do?" He whispered into Grandfather's ear. If Jake could have a secret, so could he.

Grandfather nodded. "First thing tomorrow morning. And we'll all go."

Benny beamed and claimed the last taco.

The next morning, everyone met at the desert trail. Mr. Garcia led the way. Even Mr. Tobias and Jake came along.

Violet took pictures, which she had been unable to do the night Tom Parker guided them into the desert.

Jessie strolled beside Grandfather, enjoying the cool air.

Henry kept his eyes on the ground. Finding one small gold-colored rock wouldn't be easy. But that was what Benny wanted to do, and Henry would do almost anything to make his little brother happy.

They reached the campground where Tom had built the sputtering campfire a few nights ago.

"This is probably where Benny lost his rock," Grandfather said. "Let's search the area thoroughly."

The group broke up to scour the campsite.

Benny combed the area where he had dozed off with his head on Jessie's shoulder. His rock should be right about —

"Here it is!" Triumphantly Jake held up a small rock.

"You found it!" Benny cried.

Jake dropped the stone into Benny's palm and closed his fingers around it. "Now, don't lose it again, young man. I've got to help Janine at the restaurant. See you folks later."

On the way back, Benny squeezed his fist so he wouldn't drop his rock again. When they reached the pavement, he stopped to look at his prize.

"Hey," he said. "It looks different. It's got knobs instead of square sides."

The others examined Benny's stone.

Luis whistled. "Benny! This isn't your hunk of fool's gold!"

"It's not?"

"It's the real thing! Jake gave you a genuine gold nugget."

"Wow!" said Henry. "Now we know Jake has definitely found something!"

"I think he found the mine," Jessie said firmly.

"So do I," said Luis.

Violet gazed dreamily into the brown hills. "Jake followed his heart, like the message on the stone said. I think he found good friends here. Now he won't be lonely anymore."

Benny stroked the smooth, yellow bumps embedded in the rock. Jake's present was the best souvenir in the whole state of Arizona.

"Remember when we lent Jake money?" Henry said. "And he said he'd pay us back. Well, he did."

Benny smiled broadly. "*With* interest!"

GERTRUDE CHANDLER WARNER discovered when she was teaching that many readers who like an exciting story could find no books that were both easy and fun to read. She decided to try to meet this need, and her first book, *The Boxcar Children*, quickly proved she had succeeded.

Miss Warner drew on her own experiences to write the mystery. As a child she spent hours watching trains go by on the tracks opposite her family home. She often dreamed about what it would be like to set up house-keeping in a caboose or freight car — the situation the Alden children find themselves in.

When Miss Warner received requests for more adventures involving Henry, Jessie, Violet, and Benny Alden, she began additional stories. In each, she chose a special setting and introduced unusual or eccentric characters who liked the unpredictable.

While the mystery element is central to each of Miss Warner's books, she never thought of them as strictly juvenile mysteries. She liked to stress the Aldens' independence and resourcefulness and their solid New England devotion to using up and making do. The Aldens go about most of their adventures with as little adult supervision as possible — something else that delights young readers.

Miss Warner lived in Putnam, Connecticut, until her death in 1979. During her lifetime, she received hundreds of letters from girls and boys telling her how much they liked her books.